To Hoyt,

Best Wishes
Michael Patrick Steinert

Not A Wicked Step Mother

By Michael Patrick Steiner, Sr.

NOT A WICKED STEP MOTHER

Michael Patrick Steiner, Sr.

Copyright © 1989 Michael Patrick Steiner, Sr.

STERN & STERN PUBLISHING COMPANY
ELK GROVE, CALIFORNIA
ISBN: 1-879417-00-6

I would like to dedicate this book to all the stepmothers of this world, especially my wife, Dianne. I apologize to all of you for the stepchildren who may have hurt you. They will never know what they have missed. I wrote this book with the hope that children will remember Jared Brown when they think stepmothers are wicked, or threaten the relationship with their real mother, living or dead. Please give stepmothers a chance. Believe me, you won't regret it. Love and they will love you back--and that's okay!

Remember to listen to your stepmother and remember she has a lot to teach you. When the going gets tough, she'll be there to help out.

Stepmothers, I hope this helps dispel the myth of the wicked stepmother. Remember, mothers are stepmothers and vice-versa.

With love,

Michael Patrick Steiner, Sr.

CHAPTER ONE

Hello. My name is Mary. I'm Farmer McCabe's scarecrow. Farmer McCabe says I'm the best scarecrow he has ever had because I look so real. The crows are afraid to land in the field. But it gets lonely here all day chasing crows away. If I could have two wishes, I would wish for another scarecrow for company, and the second wish would be the best of all. I would wish that we could come alive so we could talk and laugh together. Oh, how I wish this could come true!

Little did Mary know, but on that very day, Farmer McCabe was going to put a new scarecrow right next to her.

Back at the workshed, Farmer McCabe was busy getting the new scarecrow ready.

"Ah, you are just as real as Mary is," Farmer McCabe said. "The only thing you need is a name. Let me think ... Vladimir. That's it!", Farmer McCabe said with a smile.

Farmer McCabe put Vladimir into his truck, right beside him, and drove out to the field where Mary was. As Farmer McCabe drove up, Mary couldn't believe her eyes.

"Well, Mary, this is Vladimir. He is going to keep you company," Farmer McCabe said with a laugh, not knowing that Mary understood what he said.

Oh, he is so handsome! I got my wish! I got my wish!, Mary thought with excitement. Only one wish left, she thought, as she looked at Vladimir. But how? But how?

While Mary and Vladimir were getting acquainted, back in town a little boy named Jared Brown was getting ready for school.

"Hurry, Jared", yelled his father, Ben, "breakfast is ready! You can't be late for school!"

Jared ran down the stairs and sat at the table. His father said, "Remember, today you have to go to Farmer McCabe's and get the biggest pumpkin you can find for the contest I'm having at my butcher shop."

"What contest?" Jared asked.

"Well, this year, I decided to give a bike to the child who comes closest to guessing the weight of the pumpkin."

"Wow! Can I try, dad?" asked Jared hopefully.

"No, Jared. It wouldn't be fair because you are my son. Besides, you already have a new bike."

"I guess that's fair", said Jared with a half smile.

Jared grabbed his books and gave his father a hug and a kiss and walked out the door. Halfway down the path, his father yelled, "Wait a minute, Jared! Could you drop this list off to Mr. Willard at the grocery store on your way to school? It's very important.

It's a list for all the food for Ginny's and my wedding this Saturday."

Jared said yes, very reluctantly. As he walked to school he thought to himself, *why does he have to get married to her, anyway? Oh, well, I'll just think of the big pumpkin and not of the wedding. I wouldn't want to spoil a nice day.*

After Jared left for school, Ben was busy making plans for the Big Day--Saturday. Just as Ben had finished washing the last breakfast dish, a sweet voice at the screen door whispered, "Good morning, handsome".

"Come on in, Ginny", Ben said lovingly. He gave her a big hug and kiss and said, "I love you. Isn't it a beautiful day?"

"Yes, and we are the luckiest people in the world as long as we have each other", said Ginny.

"Yes, I feel the same way", Ben said as he touched Ginny's face softly. "Well, Ginny, sit down so we can finalize the wedding plans for Saturday."

"Okay", Ginny answered. "That's one of the things I love most about you, Ben, your willingness to talk things over with me."

"Well, I probably work harder to communicate than anything else I do. It was very difficult for me to do when I was younger, because in our house, there was no communication. I just wish someone--anyone--would have shared communication skills with me. My life would have been a little easier."

"Oh, Ben!" Ginny said with tears in her eyes.

"What's wrong, Ginny?"

"Nothing. Everything is all right. As you were talking, I felt even closer to you, more now than ever. Thank you for sharing part of your life with me." Then Ginny kissed Ben gently on the cheek. "I just wish Jared would find room in his heart to accept me," Ginny said sadly.

"Jared has had a rough time since his mother died. But I feel with a lot of love and

understanding and having faith in him, he will come around."

"I hope so", Ginny said, "but sometimes I think that he has already made up his mind and will never give me a chance".

"Babe, just be the same warm and loving person I love so much, and he'll see what you are offering. He'll accept it. I know he will, or he will be one unhappy little boy."

"I hope so", Ginny said. "Now, back to us. What about the flowers? What about my dress? What about the food? What about--"

"Wait a minute! Slow down, Ginny! You're starting to make *me* nervous--and I'm nervous enough already! We'll get it all together. I promise."

"Oh, Ben, you always know how to bring me back to earth--just by looking at me in your loving way."

"Let's go downtown", Ben said as he put his arm around Ginny and they walked out the door.

CHAPTER TWO

It was about two o'clock in the afternoon, and back at Farmer McCabe's pumpkin field, Mary and Vladimir had been getting acquainted all day. Still on their poles, they had been asking questions, laughing, joking and having fun.

"Do you believe in love at first sight, Mary?" asked Vladimir.

"I--I'm not too sure", said Mary blushing.

"Well, I do!" Vladimir responded enthusiastically. "When Farmer McCabe brought me up in his truck and I saw you, it was love at first sight for me!"

Mary's scarecrow cheeks turned bright red. "Oh, Vladimir!", she said.

"How do you feel about me?" Vladimir asked Mary.

With nervousness and hesitation in her voice she said, "I like you very much, Vladimir, but I just met you".

"Well, Mary, I'm a firm believer in stating how you feel, even if you have known someone for a short time. It's okay to say I love you."

"Well, then, Vladimir, I will try to express how I do feel. But first, I must tell you what I felt when I first saw you. I almost fell backwards, right off my pole!"

"Oh, really?" Vladimir said shyly. "Does this mean you really did fall in love with me the first time you saw me?"

"Yes, Vladimir. I do love you."

"Oh, that's wonderful!" Vladimir answered with love and excitement in his eyes. Then, he looked down and said, "Oh...we have company,

Mary. Look, all the animals from the forest and fields have come to visit us."

"Oh, look! All the little children are laughing and giggling. They must have heard us talking," said Mary, a little embarrassed.

"That's right", said Mrs. Coyote, as her two pups were rolling all over the ground, giggling. "Don't pay any attention to them. You know how silly kids can be over mushy stuff, but we all think you two make a wonderful couple!"

"Uh-oh. Look, Vladimir. The young mountain lion cubs are rolling pumpkins all over the field. The little rabbits are jumping from one pumpkin to another. All the other little ones are starting to get out of hand! Vladimir, do something before they ruin the pumpkins in the field! Farmer McCabe will really get mad."

Vladimir yelled as loud as he could from his pole, "Hey, everyone! Stop it!" But the little creatures didn't listen to Vladimir.

At that point, Vladimir, Mary and all the animals heard an ear piercing

10

"*WEEEOOOWHUP!!!!*" Everyone stopped dead in their tracks. They all looked up to the right, and there was Sugie Squirrel, standing on the largest pumpkin in the patch, arms folded across her chest, tapping her foot impatiently.

"Works every time", said Sugie. "Now, all you kids line up and put those pumpkins <u>back</u> where you found them, and be <u>good</u>!"

All the parent animals turned to Sugie Squirrel and thanked her once again for getting things back under control.

"You're welcome", said Sugie, then she muttered, "Give me two days, just two days, and <u>I'll</u> get these kids in shape and ready to listen to grown-ups once and for all."

After everything was back to normal, all the animals left for their homes and Mary and Vladimir just stared lovingly at each other.

CHAPTER THREE

Jared sat restless in his seat. He looked at the classroom clock. "Only ten more minutes to go. Hurry, clock," Jared whispered impatiently. "Oh, ring! Ring!" Finally, the bell sounded loudly.

As Jared started for the door, his teacher, Miss Jackie, said, "Jared, could I speak to you for a minute?"

"All right", Jared said, with a jolt, his right leg trying to go out the door and his left leg pulling him back in. "What do you want, Miss Jackie?", said Jared, forgetting his manners. "Uh, I'm kinda in a hurry. I have to go to Farmer McCabe's to get a pumpkin for my dad's butcher shop," he said clumsily, trying to be polite.

"This won't take long", answered Miss Jackie. "I want you to give this to Ginny. It is a pearl hairpin that belonged to my mother. I would like Ginny to wear it on Saturday. You know, something borrowed, for good luck."

Great. Just great, Jared thought to himself. This is what was so important I had to stay after class? "Okay, I will", said Jared as he stuffed the hairpin in his pocket and ran out the door. "'Bye, Miss Jackie!" she heard faintly from halfway down the hall. I wish he would be as excited about the wedding as he is about the pumpkin, Miss Jackie thought to herself. Ginny is my best friend. Ginny and Ben deserve to be happy. I hope Jared doesn't try to come between them. No, he won't, she thought with an uneasy feeling. He's too smart to act like that, she thought as she locked up the classroom for another day.

Jared was walking as fast as he could down Main Street on the way home. At the same time, he was thinking to himself, I guess this pin Miss Jackie gave me for Ginny is

supposed to bring her good luck. Maybe if I kind of lose it in my bedroom and not find it until Monday, she will have bad luck and the wedding will be called off. Yeah! That's what I'll do!

Honk! Honk! A horn sounded. Jared turned and saw it was his Dad, Ben, in his truck. Jared yelled in a voice like someone who got caught with his hand in the cookie jar, "Yeah, Dad! Where are you going?"

"Everything okay, Jared?", said Ben, as he pulled the truck over to the curb.

"Yes, Dad. I'm just in a hurry", Jared said, as he thought, *boy, it's a good thing he can't read my mind!*

"Jared, I'm going to the butcher shop for awhile. Tony has been there all day by himself, while Ginny and I were tying up loose ends for Saturday".

Yeah, Saturday, Jared thought to himself.

"Jared? Oh, Jared! J-A-R-E-D!"

"Yeah, Dad?"

"Your mind is a thousand miles away", Ben remarked.

"It's the pumpkin, Dad, only the pumpkin", Jared said covering his real thoughts.

"Jared, don't forget the pumpkin!"

"I won't."

"By the way, Ginny is at the house fixing you some lemonade and cookies for a snack. Why don't you stop by the house before you go."

"Okay, Dad", Jared responded.

"I've got to get going!"

"Bye, Dad."

"Bye, Jared", Ben returned. Ben sounded the horn and off he went down the street in the truck.

Jared started walking, but not hurrying. What do I do now? She's at the house! I know--I'll sneak around the bush so she won't see me. Then, I'll go in the garage through the side door. As he approached the house, he could see Ginny in the kitchen through the window. He quietly snuck around the bushes. Then, as he reached the side door of the garage, he carefully opened the door. As he felt for the light switch, Jared heard a big crash.

Ginny opened the kitchen door to the garage. "Jared, is that you? Are you all right?"

"Yeah", mumbled Jared, "I'm caught. The ladder just fell."

"Let me help you", said Ginny with a smile.

"No, I'll get it. I don't need your help."

"Okay, if that's the way you want it. If you're hungry and thirsty, I made some cookies and lemonade."

"No. I have to hurry to Farmer McCabe's. I'm already late."

"Okay, Jared, maybe when you get back."

"Maybe", Jared said.

Jared got his bike and tied his wagon to it, as he thought to himself, boy, lemonade and cookies. That sounded good. I should have said yes. Oh, well, he thought. Then off he went, down Old River Road to Farmer McCabe's pumpkin patch.

Well, I'm almost there, thought Jared as he looked up ahead and saw Farmer McCabe coming down the road on his tractor.

"Hi, there, Jared", Farmer McCabe said.

"Hi!", Jared returned with a smile.

"Did my Dad talk to you about the pumpkin I'm supposed to pick up for the contest?"

"Yes, he did, Jared, and it's all paid for so just help yourself to the biggest pumpkin you can find", said Farmer McCabe.

"Thank you", Jared said with appreciation.

"By the way, Jared, I put two new scarecrows out in the field this year. Take a look and see while you are out there."

"I will", Jared responded. "'Bye."

As he reached the field, he could see the two scarecrows in the distance. He jumped off his bike and ran across the field, jumping over pumpkins all the way. Then he stopped in his tracks, just as fast as he started. He found himself staring at the girl scarecrow. Suddenly, tears came to his eyes. With his voice cracking, Jared said, "You look just like my mother! I miss her so very much." Tearfully, Jared started talking to the scarecrow, pouring out, "She died in a car crash two years ago, all because someone we didn't know thought it was okay to drive when they had too much to drink. If only people would feel the hurt I feel, they wouldn't do things like that! And now, this Saturday, my father is getting married to that Ginny Parsons. She is nice, I guess." Then, with a lot of anger in his voice, Jared finished, "But I don't want a stepmother!" Jared reached up to touch the scarecrow's hand and a teardrop fell from his cheek. Just as he touched her hand, the tear landed there and sparkled like a shining star. Then he heard a soft voice say, "Hello, little boy. My name is Mary. What's yours?"

"J-J-Jared", he said in disbelief, his eyes wide in amazement.

"Will you unbutton my jacket so I can get down from this pole?" she asked.

A dazed Jared fumbled to undo the three buttons on the jacket.

"Oh, that's better. That coat was too hot!", said Mary. "Are you surprised, Jared?", she asked.

"Yes, I am!", he exclaimed.

"What's the other scarecrow's name?", Jared asked.

19

"His name is Vladimir", Mary answered.

Jared rushed over and touched Vladimir's hand. "He didn't come alive like you did", Jared said.

"I guess it's just not time for Vladimir to come alive", Mary said tenderly. "I'm sure when the time is right we'll all be surprised. Anyway, I heard everything you said, Jared. I am so sorry about your mother, but I cannot understand why you and your stepmother-to-be can't get along. I'm sure she loves you and your father very much or she wouldn't be marrying your father this Saturday", said Mary, trying to soothe Jared.

"She loves my father, not me", Jared said sternly.

"Have you really given her a chance to love you? It sounds to me like you have made up your mind not to even give her a chance. That's not fair to her," Mary said, tenderly.

Jared continued, "Well, she always tries to tell me what to do and what not to do. I don't like that! She is not my mother and never will be!"

"Wow! That's a pretty harsh statement about someone who is offering you love and understanding", said Mary in a surprised voice.

"Mary, I have a great idea!", Jared beamed, "Come home with me and you can be my mother!"

"Now, Jared, how could I be a better mother to you than Ginny?" Mary questioned.

"Well, you <u>look</u> like my mother", Jared responded.

Mary reached for Jared's hand, shook her head and said, "Jared, just because I look like your mother on the outside, doesn't mean I could be your mother on the inside. That's where love comes from: inside. If you love and respect people as people, and not for what you can or cannot get out of the relationship, your life will be happier. I am sure your stepmother is not trying to replace your mother in your heart. She is just trying to love you like you were her own son. She is just trying to help you become a better person. Being the new person in your family is just as hard for her as it is for you. Sometimes she might try too hard and do something you may or may not like. After all, she is only human. Forgive her, then love and respect her. She must be a good, kind, and loving person who wants to be a part of your family or she wouldn't be marrying your father. Your father and you need each other and so does Ginny."

"I never thought of it that way", said Jared.

"Well, Jared, I must go back to work, now", said Mary. "Please help me to get back up on my pole."

"Do you *have* to go now?", Jared asked.

"Yes", she replied, "but come back and tell me all about the wedding. Remember! Love and respect! Now be on your way."

As Jared stood up to leave, something stuck him in his pocket.

"Ouch! What the heck?" yelled Jared.

22

"What is it?" Mary asked.

"There's something in my pocket and it stuck me!" he said as he reached in his pocket and pulled out the hair pin Miss Jackie had given him.

"What a beautiful hairpin, Jared. Whose is it?" Mary questioned.

"It's a long story", Jared said nervously. "I'm supposed to give it to Ginny. It's from my teacher, Miss Jackie. She's Ginny's best friend. I was going to kind of lose it until Monday, but after talking to you, I think I have a better idea", Jared said with a big smile. "Mary", Jared asked, "is the old saying: 'Something old, something new, something borrowed, something blue?'"

"Yes, it is", said Mary. "Why?"

"Well, I have something borrowed, now all I need is something old, something new, and something blue. I've got it! I'll go to town. I saw a blue garter at Alice's Boutique. I'll get that for her with the money I was going to use for my fishing pole. All I need now is something old. Let me think... I know! My mother gave me an old bracelet that belonged to her grandmother. I'll give Ginny that! It's 4:30. If I leave now, I think I can make it to Alice's before she closes the store. 'Bye, Mary! I'll come see you on Monday to tell you what happened." And off went Jared, through the pumpkin field back to town as fast as he could go.

Jared reached town just in time to buy the garter for Ginny. Tonight, after dinner, I'll give it to her, he thought to himself, as Alice was putting his purchase in a bag.

"Ready for the big day?", Alice asked.

"Yes, more than ever", Jared said enthusiastically.

"It's sure nice of you to buy this garter for Ginny", Alice said.

"Well, she needed something blue and new, so I thought of this", Jared said thoughtfully.

"It's a good choice, Jared", Alice said, somewhat confused.

"Well, I've got to go, or I'll be late for dinner. Ginny's cooking my favorite tonight-- fried chicken. 'Bye", Jared said as he bounded for the door.

"What's gotten into that boy? Yesterday, he couldn't care less about the wedding. But today, it's another story. He actually is excited", Alice said to herself with a puzzled look on her face.

CHAPTER FOUR

Ben and Ginny were busy in the kitchen, getting dinner ready when Jared arrived home.

"Where's Jared?", Ben asked.

"He's been up in his room since he got home", Ginny said. "He ran through here with a bag in his hand. Haven't seen him since", Ginny added.

"Was he rude to you when you saw him?" Ben asked with concern.

"No, Ben, actually he smiled at me and was very polite. He said he had to do a few things in his room and to just call him when dinner was ready", Ginny said with some relief.

"Huh? He was?!", Ben said, wondering what was up. "I think I'll go up and see", said Ben.

"No, don't bother him, Ben. I think he wants some privacy right now. Dinner is almost ready--then you can ask him", Ginny said in a quiet, loving way.

"Okay, you're right", Ben said as he kissed her.

"Jared, oh Jared! Dinner is ready!", Ben blared up the stairs.

"Be right down", Jared called in response.

As they all sat at the table eating, Ginny asked Jared, "How was your day, Jared?"

"I had the best day of my life! How was yours, Ginny?"

"Fine", she said, kind of startled, as this was the first time he ever asked.

"I'm sorry I didn't have any cookies or lemonade this afternoon. I was just acting dumb, I guess", said Jared apologizing for his behavior earlier that afternoon.

"Apology accepted", Ginny said, still wondering what happened to this boy.

Ben interjected, "Jared, what happened to you today?"

"I guess I grew up today, a little, dad", Jared said in a tone of maturity.

"Well, what ever happened to you today, I am really happy and proud of you," Ben said in a voice of 'better leave well enough alone'.

When dinner was finished, Jared offered to Ginny, "I'll do the dishes. You and dad go in the living room and relax."

"Oh, Jared! Thank you! That's very nice of you!", Ginny said as she kissed him on the cheek.

"And after I do the dishes, I have a surprise for you", Jared told Ginny with a blush as he hugged her. "Now, go relax. Go on", Jared demanded.

"I also want to thank you, Jared", Ben said as he hugged his son. Then Ben grabbed Ginny's hand and they went into the living room.

"Ben, what's gotten into him?" said Ginny as tears of happiness filled her eyes.

"I don't know, Ginny, but I'm really curious about the surprise he has for you", Ben said with a hint of mystery in his voice.

"I'm so happy tonight, Ben. I think Jared's really trying from deep in his heart", said Ginny as she put her head on Ben's shoulder.

"Thank you, God, from both of us", Ginny said.

"Amen", said Ben.

Just then, Jared entered the room and announced, "I've finished the dishes. I'll be right back. Stay right there and don't look. Close your eyes, Ginny", Jared asked as he ran up the stairs to get the box from his room for Ginny.

As Jared came back into the room, he stood before Ben and Ginny and said, "You can open your eyes, now, Ginny". Jared was grinning from ear to ear, anticipating Ginny's delight.

"Oh, thank you", Ginny said as she accepted the box. "I wonder what it is?"

Jared beamed, "It's something you'll need on Saturday".

Ginny ripped open the present with the energy of a three year old at Christmas. As she lifted the lid off the box, she started to cry, "Jared, this is so wonderful! Can you explain each item to me? I know this garter is something blue", said Ginny, her voice still sounding surprised.

"It's also something new, because I bought it today", Jared explained. "This hairpin, Miss Jackie gave me today, is for you.   It's something borrowed. But best of all, my Mom gave this to me", Jared said as he pointed to the bracelet. "It's a gold bracelet that belonged to her grandmother, so that makes it old. So there's something old, something new, something borrowed and something blue. This means you'll have good luck", Jared said with openness and love in his eyes.

With tears in her eyes, Ginny touched Jared's face and said, "It has brought good luck already. Thank you from the bottom of my heart."

"You're welcome! And, I love you *both*. All I want now is for all of us to be happy together", Jared proclaimed.

"We both love you very much and today you've made me the proudest father in the world. Just wait until Saturday," Ben said as he smiled and put one arm around Jared and the other around Ginny. Then they all stood there hugging, filling the whole house with love.

"Sweet dreams", said Jared as he kissed them both and went off to bed.

"Sweet dreams, Jared", said Ginny and Ben in harmony.

The next morning, Ben knocked lightly on Jared's door and let himself in.

"Jared, time to get up! Come on, sleepy head! We have a lot to do before one o'clock," Ben said as he sat on the side of Jared's bed, rubbing his head tenderly.

"Dad", Jared said as he was trying to get the sleep out of his eyes, "can I ask you a question?"

"Sure."

"I know I'm the ring bearer for your wedding today, but I stayed up late last night to write a poem. Can I read it some time during the wedding? Like maybe after you say 'I do'--just before you kiss the bride?" Jared asked with a hint of "please" in his voice.

"I think that would be wonderful. I would be very proud for you to read your poem. I know Ginny will be proud, too", Ben told Jared.

"Thanks, Dad. It means a lot to me", Jared said as he jumped out of bed, pushing his father to the door. "Now, let me get ready, okay?"

"Okay", Ben answered, as he went to his room to get ready to go to the church for his big wedding day.

CHAPTER FIVE

"Hello, I am Pastor Dietch. Everyone in town is gathering today at the church. The bride is still downstairs doing last minute beauty things that women do, I suppose. 'Is my hair okay? Does my dress look good? Does my...well, you get the picture, right? I see the groom has just arrived with the best man, his partner, Tony Medrano, one of the nicest butchers in town. Boy, oh boy, Ben, you sure look nervous", Pastor Dietch said to Ben as he came into the church foyer.

"Hi, Pastor Dietch," Ben said with a dry throat.

"Are you a little nervous, Ben", asked Pastor Dietch.

"No, not m-m-me! Yes, I am. I can't lie to you. Or anyone else for that matter."

"Where's Jared", the pastor asked.

"He's coming with Ginny's parents. They just drove in from Florida this morning, and he volunteered to show them the way to the church", Ben said.

"Really? What's up with him?", asked Pastor Dietch.

"You'll see. You'll see. He's not the same boy you knew last week", Ben boasted about his son, almost popping the buttons on his shirt.

Everyone is ready to start the wedding. The church is filled with Ben and Ginny's friends and family. Flowers line the room, making it look very beautiful. Everyone is smiling. Pastor Dietch gives the signal, and the organ starts playing the wedding march: dum-dum-de-dum, dum-dum-de-dum. Ben is staring at the door at the back of the church, where Ginny appears. Ben, preoccupied with

thoughts of Ginny, doesn't even notice as Jared drops the rings while walking down the aisle. "She is so beautiful", Ben thinks to himself. "He is so handsome", Ginny thinks to herself. Ginny approaches Ben and they turn to face Pastor Dietch.

As the pastor finishes the ceremony, he proclaims, "I now pronounce you husband and wife".

Jared whispers to Ben, "Now, Dad?"

"Yes", Ben whispers back.

Jared turns to Ben and Ginny and reads them his special poem:

"When my Dad told me of your plans to wed
All I could think is *'I wish I were dead'*
Instead of dreams while lying in bed
I would think up schemes to ruin that day I dread

Then a friend came along and taught me love,
Like an angel's harp on an endless strum,
I'm sorry for having acted so dumb,
Welcome to our family, Mom!"

CHAPTER SIX

Jared jumped on his bike and raced as fast as his feet could peddle on Old River Road. As he approached the field, he could see Farmer McCabe with an old broom in his hand, shooing all kinds of animals away. There were crows, deer, rabbits and even a family of squirrels. Jared rushed over to Farmer McCabe and said, "What's happening? What's going on? How come all the animals are here?"

Farmer McCabe answered in an angry growl, "Them darned animals! Ever since the day I put the two scarecrows together, they come from everywhere and just stare at the scarecrows. They must be infatuated with the way they look or something. I just can't figure it out. Hey!", he yelled at the animals, "you're ruining my prize pumpkins!" Farmer McCabe looked up at Vladimir and Mary and spared them nothing as he shook his broom at them and shouted, "How come you two aren't scarin' these varmints away? I'm gonna have to do something about this! I guess today I'm just gonna have to go back and get my truck and take you two scarecrows back to the workshed. You stay here, Jared, and keep these animals away from my prize pumpkins until I get back here with my truck".

"Okay, I will", Jared promised.

As Farmer McCabe drove off on his tractor to get his truck, Jared ran up to Mary and touched her hand. "You've got to come alive, Mary. You have to! You just have to!", Jared begged. "Farmer McCabe will be back in a little while to take you away. You have to come alive!", Jared continued, realizing Mary wasn't coming alive. Jared didn't know what to do. He just started yelling, "I love you! I love you! You've got to come alive again! Farmer McCabe is going to take you away!" Jared reached up and grabbed Mary's hand and at the same time, he grabbed Vladimir's hand, too. He put the hands together as he said, "You both deserve to have the same kind of love that you helped me to understand." Jared just stood there, holding their hands together as his eyes swelled with tears. At that moment, two giant tear drops rolled down his cheeks. As the tears fell off his chin, they hit all three of their hands. There was a brilliant flash of light. It was as bright as the North Star. Jared raised his hands to cover his eyes because the light was so bright. As he pulled his hands away from his face, he saw that Mary and Vladimir had come alive! They smiled at him and cried out, "We're alive! We're alive!"

And Jared joined their cheer, "You're alive! You're alive!"

All the animals started celebrating. Everyone started dancing and jumping and cheering together. The rabbits danced with the squirrels. The deer sang with the crows. Mary, Vladimir and Jared held hands and danced in circles, shouting "We're alive! We're alive! Oh, thank you! The love you showed is what made all this possible!"

Then Jared turned to Mary and said, "No, you made this all possible, Mary. By showing me how to open my heart and my mind. Changing my closed mind and opening my heart to love and respect people even if I don't really know them--to give them a chance, that's what you taught me, Mary."

At that moment, Jared saw the dust rising above the road in the distance from Farmer McCabe's pick-up truck. Jared shouted, "Mary, Vladimir! You have to run! Leave! Hurry! Run! Farmer McCabe is coming!"

Jared gave them both a big hug and a kiss and said, "You have to go now. Come back and see me some time. I'll be okay now. I just want you to be free to love the way you taught me to love. So go! Run! Run and be happy!"

Jared stood and watched as Mary and Vladimir ran off into the woods. All the animals ran beside them to make sure they would find their way. As they disappeared into the bright-colored autumn trees, Jared knew in his heart they would be safe forever.

"Wait!", Jared hollered, "I didn't get to tell you about the wedding!"

"That's okay, we'll read all about it in the book", Mary replied.

Scratching his head, Jared thought, *"What book?"*

EPILOGUE

Well, two years have now passed since that first day in the pumpkin field. Jared now has a new baby brother. Even though Ginny is his stepmother, he loves her just as much as his real mother.

Mary and Vladimir got married and are now traveling and seeing the country, sharing their story about the love Jared Brown had shared with them. Mary and Vladimir decided to have a child, too. They're hoping for one just as sweet as Jared Brown.

Just for fun, try and match your photo with mine.

Love, Jared

Dear Parent,

These pages will provide an opportunity for stepparents and children to discuss and personalize *Not A Wicked Stepmother* for the new family. It is suggested that personal photos be used or the child may wish to draw pictures that may be appropriate or meaningful. For example, pictures of Dad with Stepmom, the daycare provider, the teacher, a special friend, a wedding portrait, or family outing, or some other holiday or special get-together--anything that the blended family may find appropriate to their personal situation.

It is our wish that Jared's role in *Not A Wicked Stepmother* might help smooth a bumpy road along the way. Blended families need all the help we can get!

The Editor

It is with gratitude that I happily acknowledge all those who have helped to make this book possible. Sincere and loving thanks to:

My wife, Dianne, who believed in the importance and completion of this book with unshakable love, confidence, and enduring patience;

Our children, Suzanne, Mike, Jr., Dylan, and Daniel, who helped to teach their parents the true meaning of living in a blended family and who found love from acceptance;

The Steiner, Rehfeld, and Manoguerra Families, for their support and encouragement in completing this book, especially our parents, Barbara and Bob Steiner, Sr., and Marina Manoguerra;

And to Jan Walker of Another Jan Original, for translating my "chicken scratch" into English and for her expert arrangement of the original manuscript.